The Mermaids' Ball

By Bea Sloboder
Illustrated by Heidi Petach

With best fishes to Ronnie, Victoria, Yvette,
and the rest of the great group at Grosset!—H.P.

Grosset & Dunlap • New York

Text copyright © 1998 by Grosset & Dunlap, Inc. Illustrations copyright © 1998 by Heidi Petach.
All rights reserved. Published by Grosset & Dunlap, Inc., a member of Penguin Putnam Books for Young Readers, New York.
GROSSET & DUNLAP is a trademark of Grosset & Dunlap, Inc. Published simultaneously in Canada. Printed in the U.S.A.
ISBN 0-448-41856-8   A B C D E F G H I J

All the little mermaids stretch and yawn. It's time to swim out of their oyster beds. It's time to get ready for the Mermaids' Ball!

At breakfast they sip seaweed tea, while they make
plans for a busy, busy day.

First they must go shopping for something special
to wear. Each mermaid wants to look her best for the ball.

At the Old Shipwreck Shop, they find a treasure chest.
It's filled to the brim with sparkling jewels—just the thing!

Now it's off to the coral reef. The mermaids pick out colorful coral to put in their hair. There's pretty seaweed, too, and shells of every shape and size!

After their shopping trip, the mermaids lounge in the lagoon, and take a relaxing bath in the warm water.

The waterfall is perfect for washing their long, long hair.
But they don't need to blow-dry it for an undersea ball!

Now the mermaids get dressed. They decorate themselves with all the wonderful things they have found.

How beautiful they are!

Off they go to the ball in a conch-shell coach,
drawn by six elegant seahorses.

When they arrive at the castle, the mermaid queen comes out to greet them. "Come in, come in!" she says. "The Mermaids' Ball is ready to begin!"

The orchestra plays their favorite tunes. The mermaids wave their arms and swish their tails. They dance the night away!

Dancing makes them as hungry as can be—just in time for the royal feast!
The chef dishes out delicacies from the sea—*sand*wiches, *sponge* cake, and *water*melon!

The Mermaids' Ball is drawing to a close. But first—
a grand bubbleworks display!
The mermaids watch with delight as colorful bubbles
fill the ballroom and burst over their heads.

What fun the mermaids have had at the Mermaids' Ball!